It's All about Charlie

Charlie 🐾

Kathleen Duffy
10/14

Kathleen A. Duffy

Inspiring Voices books may be ordered through booksellers or by contacting:

Inspiring Voices
1663 Liberty Drive
Bloomington, IN 47403
www.inspiringvoices.com
1 (866) 697-5313

Because of the dynamic nature of the Internet, any web addresses or links contained in this book may have changed since publication and may no longer be valid. The views expressed in this work are solely those of the author and do not necessarily reflect the views of the publisher, and the publisher hereby disclaims any responsibility for them.

Any people depicted in stock imagery provided by Thinkstock are models, and such images are being used for illustrative purposes only. Certain stock imagery © Thinkstock.

ISBN: 978-1-4624-1004-0 (sc)
ISBN: 978-1-4624-1005-7 (e)

Printed in the United States of America.

Inspiring Voices rev. date: 10/15/2014

InspiringVoices®

Chapter 1

Charlie the cat was alone. He was always alone. Not lonely ... just alone.

I like it better this way, he thought. *I can eat when I want, sleep when I want, play when I want, go where I want. Me, myself, and I are my three best friends.*

Charlie said that only to himself, of course.

The other cats and dogs stayed away from Charlie. It's not that they didn't like him. They just didn't feel they could get close to him. The other male cats around the farm liked to groom themselves and rest in the sun near the barnyard sandbox. If Charlie was there, he usually moved to another spot when any cats came near him.

Some thought he was grouchy or grumpy. Some thought he felt that he was better than anyone else, and some thought he just couldn't be bothered with the other animals. Oh, the animals talked a lot about Charlie. But whatever they thought, about anything, they *never* shared their thoughts with Charlie.

And he liked it that way. "Doesn't bother me," he would say—only to himself, of course.

You see, Charlie grew up as an "only kitten." He had no brothers or sisters. It was always just Charlie and his mother, but they were very happy together. They lived in a lovely house and were well-cared-for, indoor cats. They never went outside. Everything they needed was provided for them by their "human." That is until one, tragic turn of events changed Charlie's life forever and made him the loner that he became. But that is another story for the next book.

One day, Charlie was *very* hungry. Creeping through the tall grass and stalking his fat, juicy dinner, he heard a rustling nearby.

The rustling grew louder and nearer.

How annoying, he thought and momentarily took his eyes off his prey to see what was making the noise. Charlie's dinner took advantage of his distraction and scampered off.

The noise continued. *That does it*, thought Charlie. Turning angrily, he stomped through the grass toward the noise and roared, "Hey! Who's making all that noise? You just scared off my dinner!"

Pushing aside the long grass to see who was making the noise, he stopped breathing for a second.

Right before his eyes was the tiniest, blackest kitten Charlie had ever seen. The helpless, teeny, tiny, baby kitten was squirming around in the grass. It was not going anywhere. It was just moving around and crying.

"Mew, mew," squeaked the kitty.

"What are you doing here in *my* grass?" Charlie scolded. "Go away! I'm trying to get some dinner! Shoo! Where's your mother?"

The kitten just wiggled around a bit and mewed again.

Oh, for Pete's sake, thought Charlie. He never did have any patience with tiny kittens. Why, they couldn't even see when they were first born! That was all Charlie knew about baby kittens.

"Stop that crying! You're making so much racket that one of the dogs will surely find us," he scolded. "Where's your mother? Where's your *mother?* I certainly hope you *have* a mother! *Puh-leez* have a mother!"

The baby kitty wiggled around on the grass and continued to mew loudly! Charlie was rapidly losing patience. "*Shhhhh*, the dog will come after us with all this noise! *Shhhhhhhh!*" *I suppose I could just go and leave it here. It's none of my business what happens,* Charlie thought to himself.

Suddenly, he heard a dog barking in the distance, and it was coming closer!

"*Rats*!" cried Charlie. "That dog *is* coming this way! Well, don't just lay there! Get up and get going! What's your problem? Get up! The dog's coming! *Hurry*!"

The baby kitten wasn't paying any attention to him. It was just wiggling its legs and *still* mewing!

"Get up … get up! I'm leaving! If you don't get up right now, I'll have to go without you!"

The sound of the dog's bark was getting closer.

"Stand up! *Run!*" Charlie said as he tried to push the kitten to its feet. But the kitty's legs just folded, and it plopped back down onto the grass.

"You're going to get us killed!" Charlie hollered.

The sound of the dog became closer and closer.

Charlie decided to leave the black kitty right there. He took a few quick steps toward a big tree where he knew he would be safe from the dog.

He glanced over his shoulder. The tiny kitten was struggling and helpless in the grass.

For Pete's sake … I'll have to move it, myself. I can't just leave it here for the dog to find, Charlie thought.

Taking a deep breath, he stretched his neck, opened his mouth as wide as he could, and grabbed a mouthful of loose skin around the kitten's neck.

"Oof! That's ishgusting!" he mumbled. The kitten was *heavy*! Charlie had to stretch his neck to keep the kitten's feet from dragging on the ground and tripping him. One time, the kitty's legs got all tangled up with Charlie's front legs and down they went. *Bomp!* Landing *hard* on the ground and on the kitty, he knocked the wind out of himself.

"*Rrrwoowf! Rowf! Rrrrrrrr!*" Closer and closer came that dog.

The tree was right in front of them now.

Up! Up! Jumping on to the tree, Charlie tried to climb while carrying the extra weight of the kitten. His claws felt as though they were being pulled out of his toes. With his neck stretched forward and his jaws clamped tightly around the scruff of the kitten's neck, Charlie held the helpless kitten with all his strength and climbed.

Gotta get high enough so that stupid dog doesn't get us, he thought.

He found it! The hole in the tree that he was looking for. It was his own secret place that he used when he needed to get away from all the noise and commotion of the farm.

Charlie tried to push the tiny kitten through the hole in the tree. "Get in there! C'mon! *Oof!* C'mon, get your feet in there. Can't you even help just a little bit?"

Charlie struggled and struggled to push the limp bundle of black kitten into the hole.

By now, Charlie could hear the dog barking furiously as it ran toward them. The dog's tongue was hanging out and his mouth was wide open, showing some fierce looking teeth.

Plop! The kitten fell into the hole as Charlie clawed and stuffed himself in next to it. Finally, they were together and safe inside the tree.

Whew! Charlie was trembling and shaking. His jaw and head were pounding, da...dum! da...dum! da...dum! His heart was beating so hard that he could feel it in the tips of his ears!

Ggrrrrowlf! Rowf! Row Row Rowlf! The dog was barking and jumping up onto the tree, but Charlie and the kitten were far from his reach. The dog was noisy, but Charlie knew it would soon get bored and go back where he came from.

Time passed quickly. It became quiet now that the dog had gone.

"Well, what do you have to say for yourself?" Charlie asked the kitten. He had to speak over his shoulder because he was half sitting on the kitten and half leaning against the bumpy inside wall of the hole.

"I hope you appreciate what I just did. I had to save you *and* me—without any help from you, I might add. I'm sore, tired, and I still didn't get my dinner! Well, do you have anything you want to say to me?"

Not a sound came from the kitten.

Charlie squished himself up and twisted his already sore neck around to give the kitten his most withering glare.

It was asleep! "Harrumph," snorted Charlie. "That's gratitude for you."

Within a few minutes, an exhausted Charlie fell asleep too.

Chapter 2

Something was happening. The ground was moving!

Charlie tried to call out, "*Help*! It's an earthquake! Save me!" He opened his mouth to scream for help, but all that came out was: "*Hmpf! Fee! Hmpf! Fee!*"

Suddenly, he realized he had been dreaming. The earth wasn't moving at all. He was still sitting on that ...that ...that little, black pest! And the kitten was moving around under him.

It was dark inside the tree. Charlie tried to clear his mind. *Where are we? What's happening?*

As his groggy brain woke up, Charlie remembered and answered himself, "Oh yes. The kitten ... the dog ... the tree ... no supper." His tummy grumbled loudly. He was very, very hungry.

"Mew, mew, mew," the kitten cried.

You're probably hungry, too, he thought. Charlie knew the tiny kitty must eat, just as he, himself, had to eat.

"You stay here. I'll find us some food," he said. Untangling himself from the kitten, he squeezed out of the hole in the tree and climbed down.

Charlie thought, *It sure is warm and cozy when you are sleeping next to someone*. He shivered slightly and shook his head to get rid of that pleasant thought. *I'll feed it this once and then ... good-bye*.

The hunt was successful. Charlie had found enough food for himself and had saved some large pieces of meat for the kitty. He felt pretty good. His tummy was full, and he was bringing a nice meal to the baby.

This should make that kitty happy, he thought as he dragged the food up into the hole in the tree.

"Pssst. Where are you? Supper," said Charlie.

"Mew, mew, mew," the kitty answered.

As Charlie's eyes adjusted to the semi-darkness of the tree hole, he could see the kitten moving around. "Ah, there you are. Look, I brought you a nice meal. It's really cold out there, but I spent the extra time to drag this meat back just for you." Charlie was looking for a little gratitude. After all, if it wasn't for him, that kitten would be in big trouble.

"Here's your supper … er, breakfast by now," Charlie told the kitty as he pushed the meat toward it. The kitten sniffed at the meat and wriggled around excitedly. It kept mewing and mewing. Each mew became louder and louder. Finally, the kitten touched the meat with its tongue.

"You've got to be starving by now," Charlie said. "Go on, take a bite! What are you waiting for?"

The baby kitten couldn't or wouldn't take a bite.

"*Eat!* I'm *not* taking care of you if you starve to death!" Charlie was very upset. He had been chased by the dog, almost lost his teeth dragging the helpless kitten into the tree hole, and brought back a fine meal. Now, this thankless kitten wouldn't eat it! Just then, a thought popped into Charlie's mind. *Maybe, the kitten didn't know how to eat.*

"Here, give that meat to me. I'll show you how it's done." Charlie bit off a small mouthful of food and chewed it.

"Shee?" he said with the food in his mouth. Then he opened his mouth to show the baby what the chewed food looked like. Instantly, the baby kitten stuck its face into Charlie's mouth and licked some of the food!

"Pffttttt!" Charlie spat out the food in the direction of the kitty. "*Yuck!* What'd you do that for?" Immediately, the kitten started to gobble up the small, mushed-up pieces of chewed food.

11

Charlie squeezed his eyes tightly shut. The sight was totally offensive to him. *I can't watch this*, he thought. But he knew the tiny kitten would need more than that one mouthful of food. The only way the baby could eat the meat was if Charlie "prepared" it for him.

"Mew, mew, mew." The baby's cries were becoming more and more desperate. It needed more food, and it needed the food now.

"Okay, okay, give me a minute to get it ready." Charlie repeated the bite and chewing procedure and quickly spat out the food in a small pile near the baby until the whole piece of meat was gone. It really wasn't so bad, if he kept his eyes closed. He opened them just a crack to make sure the food was in a neat pile and the kitty was still eating. If this was the worst thing he had to do to keep the kitty alive, well, he could do it. But, just this!

While the baby was finishing, Charlie thought to himself. *It sure was hungry. I'll bet that kitten wouldn't have lasted much longer without me.*

The kitten had food all over its face. Liking his world neat and tidy, Charlie decided to help the kitty clean up a bit by licking the excess food pieces off of its face. That way, he wouldn't be offended when he looked at it. He licked the baby's face very gently. Its fur was so soft and came clean faster than he thought it would. Charlie gave a few extra licks to the kitty's face.

"Purrrrrr, purrrrrr, purrrrrr," responded the baby.

Hmmmm, thought Charlie, *finally a noise other than crying!*

Chapter 3

Charlie let out a deep sigh and felt his body relax for the first time in two days. At last, he had some peace, and quiet. The baby kitty appeared to be asleep. Charlie realized there was nothing to do now but close his eyes and get some rest.

Charlie's nose began to twitch a bit, then his nose began to wiggle. *What's that funny smell? I didn't notice that before*, Charlie thought.

He leaned over and sniffed the sleeping kitty. "Oh no! You didn't!"

Poor Charlie! He had forgotten the one rule of digestion: "What goes in ... must come out," Baby kitty had reminded him.

Now what do I do? Charlie thought to himself. The kitten was in a deep sleep and somebody had to clean up the mess. Charlie was not only tired from all of his adventures, he was exhausted from thinking about somebody else and working so hard for somebody else. When he saw the mess, he felt like crying. To make matters worse, it was beginning to rain.

Charlie took a deep breath (well, not too deep), shook away his tears, and began to work out a plan in his mind. *First, I've got to clean up this mess.*

With a few well-aimed kicks from his hind legs, the "mess" was knocked out of the tree hole. *Now I have to get some type of bedding in case this happens again.* Down the tree he scampered. Between large raindrops, he pulled up mouthfuls of sweetgrass and clover and brought them into the tree hole to use as a lining for the bottom. Again and again, he carried the grasses, leaves, and clover up the tree and into the hole to make a thick floor beneath the kitty. Charlie was building a nest!

As he was getting pelted with large, cold, rain drops, his mind was crabbing and complaining while he worked. *I look just like a squirrel. Running up and down this foolish tree and carrying a bunch of leaves in my mouth. Nobody better see me.* Charlie had no use for squirrels. He had many opinions about squirrels and was not afraid to speak them if anyone asked. They were "uncivilized." They were too noisy with all their chatter. They had no manners; and he hated their "rough and tumble" type of playing and chasing each other.

Beside that behavior ... they steal, he thought to himself. Charlie knew squirrels would steal. He saw one digging up an acorn that another squirrel had hidden. That was all the proof he needed. *The only good thing about squirrels,* he thought, *is they are hard workers.* Charlie knew that gathering nuts, seeds, and acorns for winter was hard work, and he respected hard work. And he, too, certainly was working hard.

Carrying up his last mouthful of clean grasses, the sky opened up and the rain came down in buckets. Now, he had a nice, thick mattress of grasses and clover under himself and the baby kitty.

"Good idea," he said out loud. The bedding was thick enough so that if, and when, another "accident" happened, he would remove the soiled area and still have a clean layer underneath.

Charlie rearranged some of the grasses, spread them out smoothly, and settled in beside baby kitty to try, again, to rest. It was very cozy inside the tree hole. He was warm and dry with a sleeping baby kitty snuggled up next to him. Charlie closed his eyes and listened to the pitter-patter sound of the rain against the tree and the soft sounds of baby kitty breathing. Feeling the warmth of the kitten's body beside his own, he let out a long sigh. "Ahhhhh, this is nice." And they slept.

Chapter 4

Four days had passed since Charlie found the baby kitten. Kitty seemed to be doing okay. It ate whatever Charlie brought home and appeared to be getting stronger although that was hard to tell in the low light of their tree-hole house.

Charlie, himself, was not doing as well as the kitten. He was *exhausted* and almost at the end of his rope.

I haven't had a full night or day's rest since I found it, he thought to himself. Hunting enough food for two, feeding the baby kitty, cleaning up the baby's mess, giving the baby kitten a bath each day, making both of them comfortable and safe, and going up and down the tree with clean bedding every day or so—he was really tired.

In addition to all the tiring work, the bad weather was wearing him down. What had started as a nice summer shower had not stopped for three days. Rain, rain, and more rain. It was still pouring rain, and he knew the baby kitty needed more food. If he was alone, he would just have turned over and gone back to sleep and ignored his tummy's rumbling as long as he could. But the baby was mewing very softly. Charlie was afraid it might get weak.

Charlie had been thinking and thinking about his problem. *I can't keep this up by myself. I need some help.*

How did I ever get myself into this? he wondered. *My life has been turned upside down. Oh, how I wish someone else could help me with all this work. And I wish there was someone other than me to care for baby kitty. But it's me ...just me ...and me alone!* Sighing heavily, he left his dry, warm "nest" and climbed down the tree. Once again, he set out into the cold rain to find food for baby kitty. Charlie *hated* the rain. It was so cold and made his fur clump together and get matted. Ugh!

There's nothing to hunt out here in the rain, Charlie realized. *I'll go over to the farm and see what the barn cats are eating. Maybe, I'll find some leftovers.*

Charlie ran through the grass to the barn as fast as his heavy, soaked fur coat allowed. As he moved toward the barn, Charlie had a brainstorm. *I'll see if one of the mother cats will take the baby kitty! Why didn't I think of that before? I'll just bring it here and leave it for one of them to find! Charles* (he always called himself by his formal name)*, you are a genius!* That would solve everything. The other cats had lots of babies ...all the time. What difference would one more make? He'd unload the baby kitten and get on with his life. *Freedom!* he thought. *I'll have my life back!*

Of course, it'll have to be a good mother. It must be one that would take good care of the baby kitty ...

No problem, all mothers are the same, he assured himself.

Chapter 5

When he arrived in the barnyard, Charlie spied a large puddle of freshly spilled milk. He immediately drank his fill. Out of the corner of his eye, he saw two mother cats drinking from the same puddle. He followed the thin, rather tired-looking, black-furred cat who looked like she could be baby kitty's mother.

She'll never notice another kitten, thought Charlie, *especially one that looks like her.* He quietly stayed behind the mama cat and noticed that she was full of milk. *I'll bet that she's a good mother.*

He watched as she plopped herself down on her side. From out of nowhere exploded at least six kittens. It seemed more like forty kittens to Charlie, but he only counted six. They pushed and shoved one another out of the way to get at their mother. Charlie was shocked at their behavior! Some of the bigger kittens hissed and spit at the smaller ones to frighten them away. The large kittens settled in to nurse, leaving the smaller ones to cry hungrily.

The commotion, the shoving and pushing, the crying, the fighting! *Why doesn't that mother control the ruffians? These kittens were behaving as badly as ... as ... as squirrels!* Charlie thought with a shudder.

While Charlie stared at the feeding frenzy, he noticed the mother cat's face. She looked worn out. Her fur was shabby and thin in spots. She just closed her eyes to the ruckus.

"I'll bet she doesn't have a minute to herself." Charlie muttered under his breath.

Baby kitty would never survive in that family. Those big kittens would probably get all the food leaving his little friend with nothing.

"No. Not this family," Charlie decided.

Leaving the barn, Charlie spotted the other mama cat.

She's more lively and young, he noticed. *She's not black colored, but she might do fine*.

Keeping a good distance from the mama cat, Charlie followed her to the front porch of the farm house. Squeezing through the lattice, she settled in the dirt under the porch floor.

This might be the one, Charlie thought.

Only three babies were feeding, but something wasn't right. The mother stopped the kittens from feeding after just a short time. She even pushed them away when they tried to go back for more milk. These baby kittens didn't look well. They were thin and covered with dirt from under the porch.

Hmmm, my baby kitty looks healthier than they do, Charlie thought proudly. *I've seen enough! These other mothers don't know how to care for their babies. I'm doing better than they are!* **My** *baby kitty is clean and well fed.* **My** *baby kitty will learn manners,* Charlie said haughtily to himself. *They're all just low class barn cats. At least, I came from a long line of well-bred house cats.* All the way back to the tree-hole house, Charlie was thinking about the baby kitty. He was pleasantly surprised at how much he anticipated seeing the kitten. Just thinking about it brought a smile to his whiskers. Once he decided that the baby kitty would stay with him, not just for now, but for always, something happened to Charlie. On the outside, he looked just the same. But on the inside, he felt *bigger.* And he experienced a brand-new feeling when he thought about the kitten. His heart felt warm and soft. At first, Charlie thought it was indigestion, but he hadn't eaten anything. This new sensation stayed with him while he found a quick supper for the baby and ran through the rain to the nest in the tree hole.

Charlie popped his head into the opening, dropped the food, and squeezed himself inside. He was happy to be out of the rain. He was even happier when his eyes fell on the dark shape of the baby kitty sleeping in a corner. Charlie tiptoed around the small space and made a nice pile of "supper" for the kitten. Then he very gently rubbed the side of his face along the length of the kitty in the way that cats do to show that something belongs to them. Charlie was purring all the while.

With a helpless baby kitten as his teacher, Charlie was learning that life is *not* all about Charlie. It is all about love.

And the best is yet to come.

About the Book

This is the first in a series of "Charlie" books. When Charlie the cat rescues an orphaned kitten, his life begins to change in ways he never, ever expected. Along with more responsibility comes making new friends, sharing his feelings, and best of all, giving and receiving unconditional love.

In Charlie's next adventure, he discovers his kitten is a girl and he experiences many concerns shared by single, human parents. Did he do the right thing in keeping her? Will he be able to provide for her and keep her safe? Will she be happy with him? What will their future bring? Charlie reluctantly opens up and shares his feelings and worries with some of the other male cats at the sandbox. As we learn more about Charlie's past, he continues to progress toward losing his taciturn, curmudgeonly ways. He even becomes best friends with Mrs. Squirrel, who gives him advice on kitten rearing.

The theme of this series is love (in all its many forms), acceptance of others, and the practice of not judging.

About the Author

Kathleen A. Duffy is a nurse, wife, mother of three, and grandmother to four boys. The "Charlie" books are based on her relationship and adventures with her dear friend of more than twenty-seven years ... the real-life, human Charlie.

CPSIA information can be obtained
at www.ICGtesting.com
Printed in the USA
BVXC01n0432181114
375568BV00003B/3